FRANKLIN'S FLYING BOOKSHOP

JEN CAMPBELL

illustrated by
KATIE HARNETT

Thames & Hudson

Franklin loves stories.

Stories keep him warm at night.

His front door is a bookcase that keeps out the wind.

There are lots of books inside the cave that Franklin lives in.
He likes to read them out loud for everyone to hear.

Every day, Franklin reads about King Arthur and roller skating,

about electricity and baking.

He reads about spiders

and ballet ...

... and how to do kung fu.

When the sun goes down, Franklin reads by the light of a thousand fireflies
(because fireflies like to hear stories, too).

But if it's a warm night, he spreads his wings
and flies into the sky to read by the light of the moon.

There is a village near Franklin's cave.
Sometimes Franklin goes there
but it is always quiet and it is always empty
and he can never find anyone to read stories to.

So Franklin goes home and reads about gymnastics
and helps the bats in his cave set up a trapeze.

Then he yawns very loudly and stretches his tail
and climbs into bed with a cup of camomile tea.

He sleeps tucked up under hundreds of comics
and dreams about Vikings sailing over the sea.

One day, by the stream,
Franklin sees a man.
'What are you?' cries the man,
quaking in his boots.

'I'm Franklin!' says Franklin,
and he holds out his hand.
'I'm a dragon who loves books
and I live in a cave.'

But the man drops his fishing rod and runs far away.

So Franklin goes home and reads about music
and helps the mice in his cave start up a band.

Next day, by the farm, Franklin sees a lady.
'What are you?' cries the lady, shivering on the spot.
'I-I'm Franklin,' says Franklin, and he holds out his hand.
'I'm a dragon and a band manager and I like ballet.'

But the lady screams loudly and runs far away.

So Franklin trails home and reads about space
and helps the fireflies make patterns like the stars in the sky.

Next day, in the woods, Franklin sees a young girl.

She has bright red hair,
        the same colour as the leaves,
and she's reading a book
        sitting under a tree.

'Who are you?' asks the girl, jumping up to her feet.

'I-I-I'm Franklin,' says Franklin,
and he holds out his hand.
'I'm a dragon who likes stargazing
and playing croquet.'

'I love dragons!' cries the girl,
and she shakes Franklin's hand.

'You're in this book that I'm reading
about a faraway land.'

Luna tells Franklin she's read about remote secret islands,
about treasure hunts and pirates,
about fruit bats and acrobats and how to be a spy.

Franklin tells Luna he's read about sword fighters and fire-eaters,
about circuses and anteaters,
about flower arranging and carol singing and making apple pie.

Luna and Franklin feel like they are made out of stories.

Stories with exciting beginnings, thrilling middles, and very happy ends.
Stories about new people and strange places and about making friends.

so they sit down together and come up with a plan.

They hoist bookshelves up high with the help of the mice
and tie ropes round and round to make sure they fit tight.

They move a sofa, some cake tins, tie comics on with string ...

... to make a small, lopsided bookshop between Franklin's wings.

Everybody climbs on board.

Luna holds her breath. The mice hold each other.
The fireflies gasp and the bats cross their toes.

Franklin bends down low and runs as fast as he can.

He sprints down the hill and spreads out his wings,
and takes off into the sunset with the help of the wind.

Franklin lands his flying bookshop
in the middle of the village.

'It's that dragon!' cries the fisherman.
'What a monster!' another cries.

'His name is Franklin!' shouts Luna,
a fierce look in her eyes.

'We built this bookshop together
from the books in his cave.
Franklin's kind and he's clever
and he is my friend.'

There is a small silence.

Franklin shuffles his feet in the quiet street.

'It's nice to meet you,' he says, as he waves at the crowd,
who have stopped in their tracks and are listening now.

'We have lots of stories that we'd love to share.
Please come say hello and pull up a chair.'

The fireflies light up the shelves.

The bats cartwheel along the bookcases.

And the mice clear their throats and start singing songs.

It isn't long before the villagers start taking a look,
climbing up on to Franklin to peer at the books.

Franklin takes a deep breath as Luna passes out cake.
He tells them stories about scientists and Antarctica and snakes.

He whispers tales about dragons, and how to make crème brûlée.
And everyone is listening to what he has to say.

'Let's fly,' Luna smiles, as the fireflies dance
and the acrobatic bats show off their kung fu.

So they all hold on tight, as Franklin takes flight,
reading books by the light of the moon.

'For Ollie & Phoebe' – Jen Campbell
'For my family' – Katie Harnett

First published in the United Kingdom in 2017 by Thames & Hudson Ltd,
181A High Holborn, London WC1V 7QX

First paperback edition published in 2018

Franklin's Flying Bookshop © 2017 and 2018 Thames & Hudson Ltd, London
Text by Jen Campbell © 2017 and 2018 Thames & Hudson Ltd, London
Illustrations by Katie Harnett © 2017 and 2018 Katie Harnett

British Library Cataloguing-in-Publication Data
A catalogue record for this book is available from the British Library

ISBN 978-0-500-65171-1

Manufactured in China by Imago

To find out about all our publications, please visit **www.thamesandhudson.com.**
There you can subscribe to our e-newsletter, browse or download our
current catalogue, and buy any titles that are in print.